FEEDING MINDS:

A Collection of Prose and Poetry inspired by the Visual Verse prompts

by Ekaterina Crawford

The Ninth Gate Publishing

Books That Take You Places

Published by The Ninth Gate Publishing, 2023
Copyright © 2023 Ekaterina Crawford
Cover design – Ekaterina Crawford

A CIP catalogue record for this book is available from British Library.

ISBNs:

Paperback: 978-1-912696-05-5
Kindle: 978-1-912696-04-8

The Ninth Gate Publishing
120 Baker St.,
London, W1U 6TU

For my sons

My inspiration

My creative force.

Love you lots.

Always.

Mum

A foreword and acknowledgements

First of all, please, allow me to thank you.

You holding this collection in your hands means a lot to the aspiring writer. It truly does.

Whether you have been gifted this book or purchased one, I'm grateful that you have decided to entrust me with the most precious thing you have – your time. So, thank you!

Creative pieces collated in this collection have been written over the period of several years, starting from 2019 – each inspired by the visual prompt offered by the Visual Verse Anthology.

What is the Visual Verse you ask?

Visual Verse was a creative collaboration of artists and writers – a challenge to use a visual prompt as a springboard, and, *within one hour*, to write, edit, and submit a poem or a flash fiction of 50 to 500 words.

Trust me, when you think that one hour is a long time to come up with something clever within a specified wordcount, it really isn't. In reality, this hour runs away from you before you even know it. But, in all fairness, it's great fun! And the most amazing part of it is how each individual writer takes on a challenge of the visual prompt, interprets what they see in their own personal way, and how many completely different pieces come out at the end!

Some of the works in this collection – like the title piece "FEEDING HUNGRY MINDS", the last fiction "WEIGHING OUT THE OPTIONS", and (you will be surprised) "MINUTES OF THE EXTRAORDINARY MEETING OF THE "CLAWS AND WHISKERS SOCIETY" can qualify as a life writing, as have been inspired by the true events.

"WHEN PIGS CAN'T FLY, THEY SWIM" inspired by my younger son and his unconditional love for pigs, as well as his habit to constantly play "Knock-knock. Who's there?". Now, he has, thankfully, grew out of the latter, but he still adores his pigs.

"13.1 – ONLY HALF CRAZY" is dedicated to my forever running buddy Liz. She's the best sport!

Other pieces are original ideas inspired solely by visual prompt that accompanies them.

Unfortunately, the Visual Verse has now wrapped up its creative collaboration, but I'm privileged to have been a part of it for the past five years, to have seventeen of my original works published by their Anthology and to have been invited to be a featuring writer for one of their last issues. My only regret is that I didn't know about the Visual Verse sooner.

If you've never came across the Visual Verse, this collection will be different to what you might expect, but I promise you it will be funny and refreshing, sometimes even strangely glorious, beautiful, sometimes sad, sometimes totally bonkers, but most importantly honest.

Because each creative piece was written in response to the visual prompt, this collection would not have existed without the beautiful and challenging artwork that was generously offered by the artists, and I think it's important to say thank you to them as well.

And a special thanks to those who allowed me to use their beautiful works, as some of the creative pieces wouldn't make any sense, and I do mean it, unless accompanied by the visual prompt that inspired it.

And the last, but not least, a huge thanks to my creative writing teacher Lisa McKinnon – who first introduced me to the Visual Verse and to all my creative writing buddies from Kingston Adult Education Centre for their guidance and direction, constant encouragement, and the words of wisdom.

I hope it all makes sense. And if it doesn't, I hope it will make at least some sense once you get to the end of this little book.

So, make yourself a cup of tea, or a coffee, or perhaps a cup of something a little bit stronger, get comfortable in that favourite chair of yours and enjoy. And if you really like it, feel free to leave me a little review on Amazon or Goodreads.

Thank you!
With lots of love,
Ekaterina

LOST RACE

1950s/1960s
    Sputnik 1 and Sputnik 2,
        the first living creature in space,
            the first man orbits the earth.
          Space race won.

Late 1960s/1980s
    You've sent a woman into space,
        But it was Armstrong who reached the moon.
            Apollo-Soyuz test project – a historical handshake.
          You're falling behind in the race...

Your domination,
once profound,
now, is only laughable
attempt to thrive,
more like to survive.
Industry's robbed and corrupt.
Livelihoods destroyed,
lives wrecked, yet
government secrets
are protected and
the patriot's heads
are still lifted high up.

2019
    Gagarin's "poyekhali"
      is muffled
        by the Crew Dragon's
       loud roar.
        SPACE.
        RACE.
         LOST.

MASTER JERRY'S GARDEN

Image by Craig Carry*

Master Jerry, quite contrary,
How does your garden grow?

With sadness and tears and diamond rings,
That's how my garden grows.

Master Jerry, quite contrary,
When will your garden bloom?

When she will accept me and say that she loves me,
And when I'll become her groom.

But she doesn't want me.
Entranced by own beauty,
She spends her days by the lake.

Her hair brown as a turn soil,
Her eyes blue as heavens,
But her soul is the one a snake.

She says she will love me
When I'll bring her a fern flower,

And an acorn from an old dead oak.

And so, I must wander
To beyond and yonder
To search for love and hope.

* **Craig Carry** *is an illustrator, designer and printmaker based in Cork, Ireland. Craig's commercial work includes producing work for the arts, music and book publishing sectors; including creating gig posters, album covers and book covers. Over the years, his screen printed gig posters have been made for many musicians and bands including: Courtney Barnett, Feist, Glen Hansard, Wilco, Willy Mason. Artwork on album covers include independent record labels such as: Domino, Memphis Industries and Sonic Cathedral; as well as musicians including: Bell X1, Cheval Sombre and HousePlants.*
https://www.instagram.com/craigcarry/

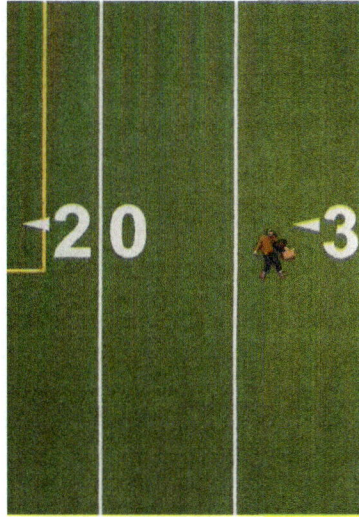

JOINING YOU

Lying on my back, I stare into the darkening heavens.

The April's evening is cold, yet I remain motionless, knowing that just in a few minutes my body will stop feeling the earth's frosty fingers that are digging in through the layers of my clothes.

People here are nicer to me now. Now that they know my story, they no longer see me as this strange, disturbed person, they no longer call the police, no longer try to remove me from the stadium.

Year after year, I return here on the same day of the same month and lie on this very spot. The spot where you've been taken away from me.

Some say, it gets easier with time. But those who say it have, obviously, never grieved. It didn't get better. It just doesn't. Not after five years, nor even after ten, nor even now.

I no longer kick and scream though, which, I guess, is a progress. And I no longer cry. I just stay here until the sky grows completely black and the bright night starts beginning to dance before my eyes, rearranging themselves into random shapes. Forming your face.

You look down at me from your heavenly home. Smiling. You always smile. Always have. I look back at you and with each passing minute, I slowly slip further and further away into the cold blackness.

"I'll be soon, my darling. Wait for me. I'll be joining you very soon."

LULLABY

Bottles are white, dilly, dilly
Bottles' lids are red
Skies are so blue, dilly, dilly
Light clouds are as soft as bed.

But it will end soon, dilly, dilly
Plastic's around
There's a hole in the Ozone, dilly, dilly
The skies will black out.

Saving our Earth, dilly, dilly
We'll save ourselves
Our planet's just one, dilly, dilly
It can't protect itself.

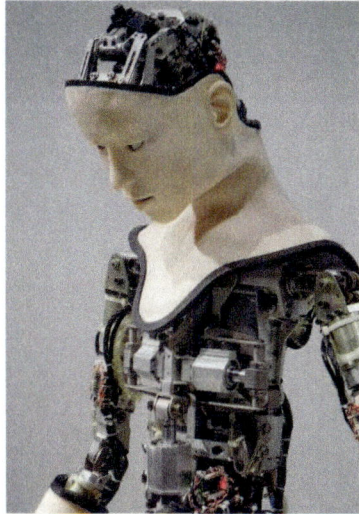

SAVE OUR SOULS

We lose ourselves
In the whirlpool of digitisation.
We lose touch,
When Insta-messages replace conversation.
We lose feel,
When likes replace hugs.

Twitter to Tinder,
Instagram to Telegram,
We lose our identities.
Trying to become someone else,
We gradually lose ourselves
to our virtual duplicates.

Bit by bit, kilobyte to megabyte,
Gigabyte to terabyte
We are digitalising.
Eyes – flashing diodes.
Veins – coloured wires.
Brains – 28-Core Monster 5GHz processors.

We're drowning.
We're fading away.

Our souls shrinking,
in proportion to our growing following.
Who will be able to find us
if we're all lost.

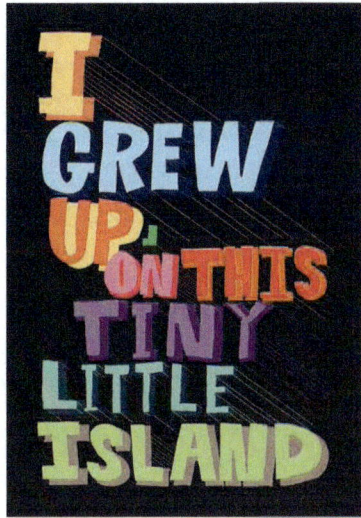

DESERT ISLAND SURVIVAL

Image by Rude Ltd*

"Are you sure these are OK to eat?" She wrinkled her nose.

"Best I could find," he shrugged.

"Maybe, if you look in those bushes, you find some berries or fruits. Maybe?"

"If you don't know what you're picking, berries could be poisonous. These, at least, I know are safe."

"Not sure my stomach can take these maggots."

"They're snails."

"Whatever they are, they look disgusting!" she said, as her face acquired light green shade. "I wish I brought snacks."

"It's a desert island survival experience! We must learn to survive in the wild. With what we have. Besides, you don't have to eat it raw. We can make them into a soup!"

"Something tells me you're not joking."

"Of course I'm not! Wait here!" he said with a mischievous

twinkle in his eye and disappeared into the greenery. He returned soon carrying a pile of twigs and dry leaves and, producing from the pocket a magnesium fire starter, got to business. Holding her breath, she watched as the hot sparks landed into the makeshift campfire. In a few flicks, little flame began to kindle, slowly growing in size and heat.

"Wow!" she exhaled. "Where did you learn to do that?"

He beamed at her but didn't reply. Disappearing into the trees again he returned with more wood and the old, rusted pot filled with water.

"Where did you get that?"

"It washed up onto a shore half a mile from here. And I found a freshwater stream close by!" he declared proudly, fixing the sticks up and hanging the pot over the flame.

When the water boiled, he threw in some dry roots, leaves and finally snails, and an hour later, their feast was ready.

"Ladies first," he smiled, filling the wooden spoon he whittled just now, with a dark thick substance.

"Is it too late to become vegetarian?" Her lips quivered.

"Don't be daft! They're high in protein. It'll keep you full for longer."

"I don't really feel that hungry...maybe you eat first and–,"

"C'mon, Steph, you can do it!" he encouraged.

She braced herself, opened her mouth and squeezed her eyes very tight.

As a saving grace, her mum's voice came from the neighbouring garden.

"Stephanie! Your lunch is ready!"

"Oh," she exclaimed, relieved and slightly disappointed. "Sorry, Adam. Have to go."

"Sure. You will come tomorrow. Right?"

"Of course! Coming, Mum! I liked your Robinson Crusoe game!" Her eyes smiled.

"Thanks." He blushed, looking at his worn-out trainers.

"Playing with you is much more fun than playing with other boys. David is silly most of the time."

"Thanks, Steph. You're pretty cool too. For a girl."

She smiled, looked away and then leaned forward and awkwardly brushed her lips against his cheek.

"Read more books," she whispered before she ran away.

RUDE *was founded 25 years ago by Rupert & Abi Meats. As trained graphic designers they launched a t-shirt label which soon grew into a creative street brand. RUDE''s reputation soon earned them commissions as graphic artists, often commissioned for their colourful hand drawn typography. Abi heads up mural work and animation projects and also looks after their Art & Coffee Shop 'Everyday Sunshine'. Rupert draws and creates original artwork for the shop and for project commissions.*
www.thisisrude.com; IG: rude.studio

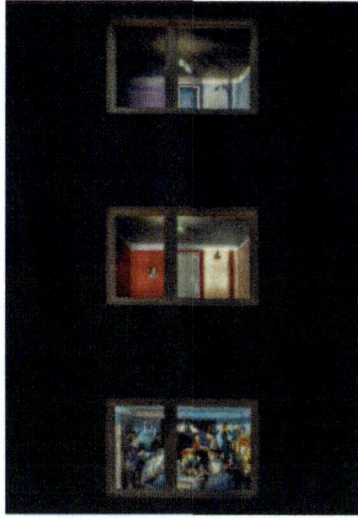

Image by Joelle Chmiel
Public domain

THE HOUSE THAT LOVE BUILT

Young love —
sweet intoxication
loud and bright,
wild and liberate.
It opens its heart freely.
Welcomes anyone.

It grabs fast.
Burns fast. Burns bright.
It's smoke, a light cloud,
changes direction
with each puff of a wind.

Seasoned love —
Cautious.
It chooses it circles more carefully
Probing, planning, hoping.
It looks for perfection
and can't quite find it.

Weathered love
is private. Secluded.
Lights dimmed
and curtains drawn.
Hidden from praying eyes,

its savoured slowly.

Withstood the test of life,
it belongs to those,
who don't need grand parties
or loud celebrations,
to those who cherish it's every flaw
and enjoy even the most bitter taste to the full.

DRESSMAKER

Image by Tanya Layko
(Таня Лайко). Public domain

Eyes glued to the screen of her phone, thumbs raining over the keyboard, as a wild summer storm, Jane marched into the kitchen. She stumbled over the cardboard box by the wall, hopped on one leg and muttering curses collapsed onto a chair.

Finishing her message and sending it flying through the internet universe, she slammed the phone onto the table.

"Is everything all right?" her mother asked.

"How could she do this to me?!" Jane stated at her mother. "How? We have agreed, right? We take a year off to travel. And then we go to Uni. Together!"

"Angela?"

"Who else! Treacherous -,"

"Language!"

"What? She now sends me this message that she met this boy, who's in Spain and that she wants to study there! In Europe! And what am I supposed to do?"

"There. There." Her mother sat on a chair next to her, hugged Jane and patted her back gently. "I'm sure if you leave it for a few days, you'll be able to clear things up."

"Whatever." Jane wiggled out of her mother's embrace and rubbed her bruising toe. "What's in the box, anyway? A pile of bricks?"

She heaved the box onto the table.

"It's Nana's," said her mother. "The Home sent it."

"What now? It's been what? Six? Seven months?"

"Eight, actually. They just found it. And all things considered, I think, the timing is perfect."

Jane gave her mother a look, opened the box and took out one of the A3 albums stacked in a neat pile.

She flipped through the pages filled with sketches of models, with various pieces of fabric attached to them.

"Did Nana do these?" Jane run her fingers over the patch of silk shaped into a skirt.

"She did."

"Mum! These are amazing!"

"They are," her mother sighed, tears looming in her eyes. "Nana might have forgotten us or her own name, but she has never forgotten this."

She touched a piece of tartan wool, shaped into a coat over a figure sketched in pencil.

"Nurses said that in the last few years, it was the only thing that kept her grounded. Re-connected to her old shelf."

"These are beautiful!" Jane looked through the pages.

"She always made our clothes. She was rather good at it, actually."

"I can imagine! These designs are really cool. Did she ever study or take it further? I mean like a professional career?"

"Study? No. She picked it up as she did alternations for friends and neighbours. I'm sure she would have wanted to make a career out of it, but when dad died, with the five of us she hardly had time for anything else. You on the other hand."

Jane's eyes lit up.

"You were always great at making clothes for your dollies."

"Kingston University has one of the best Fashion courses!" Jane exclaimed.

"How convenient." Her mother smiled.

"And I can call my fashion brand "Nana's Sewing Box". She beamed. "I'm gonna call Angela, she's gonna love it!"

WHEN PIGS CAN'T FLY, THEY SWIM

Image by Jakob Owens
Public domain

– Oink-oink.
– Who's there?
– Oink-oink, oink-oink!
– Our mates are in the air?

– Oink-oink!
– How come they fly?
– Oink-oink, oink-oink!
– What do you mean, they're falling from the sky?

– Oink-oink, oink-oink...
– Oh, for the love of bacon, can you speak normal, please!
– Sorry, what I mean is...

Trying to avoid being slaughtered for breakfast,
Our maties have legged it and headed for exit.
But they've quite forgotten the barn's on a cliff...
– OH, NO! They're all dead!

– Dead? As if!
They twisted and tumbled and then turned around
They somersaulted, flipped and...
– Splat on the ground?

– Oh no, they're quite safe.
They've ended up in the ocean.
I'm literally here to pick up sun lotion.
– …………

– They're having a pool party!
And I suggest that you come
Unless you want to be that piggy
Who stayed at home…

So, covered in sun cream, with trunks on my shoulder,
I march to the beach and dive in from the boulder.
I splash in warm water, squeal at the top of my lungs,
And hope that sun won't burn my pink little buns!

TIRED OF THE NEWS, TIRED OF THE NET,
TIRED OF ANXIETY, TIRED OF REGRET.
SO I FELL ASLEEP AND DREAMED
I WAS A LEOPARD MADE OF MIDNIGHT CLOUDS
AND THE BRIGHT MOON SHONE THROUGH ME

STARGAZING

Image by Omar Musa
Public domain

"Mum! The light is doing it again!" He shouts from the garden.

I stir the hot chocolate into two thermos mugs and walk out. The motion activated light blinds me as I step through the doors.

"Right. I see what you mean."

I place the mugs onto the wooden garden table and pull out the phone.

While I fiddle with the light settings, he vanishes into the house. When he stumbles back out through the French doors it's pitch black. You can barely see him behind a mountain he's carrying – a pillow and a duvet, a couch cushion and a heavy tartan blanked.

"Oh! well done, Mum!"

"Thank you. Not bad for your old Mama!" I laugh.

"You're not old," he says with authority, making himself comfortable in a hammock. "You just need a bit of catching up on the tech side."

"Tech side was always your dad's domain."

"Yeah. I know." He says, and I wish I could see his face right now.

I pass one of the thermos mugs over to him and climb onto the table. The old wood wobbles and creaks as I settle, tuck the cushion under my head and pull the blanket over.

He sips his drink, and as our eyes adjust to the dark, gradually, the stars begin to pop across the velvety blackness.

"Look!" He points up. "The Big Dipper!"

"You're right! What about that one?" I point at the group of stars that look like the letter "W".

"That's Cassiopeia. And those three bright stars over there, it's Orion's belt."

"Wow! You do know your constellations."

"I learned from the book dad gave me for my birthday," he says a bit hesitantly.

"Well done! What else can you see?"

He goes quiet, eyes fixed on the black sky.

"Well. If you draw a line from that star in the Big Dipper, all the way up, you'll find Polaris."

"Polaris?"

"Yeah, the North Star. Wow! Did you see that?" He sits up. "Did you see the shooting star?"

"Yes. Yes, I did."

"Too fast to make a wish, huh!"

He climbs out of his hammock, takes his pillow and duvet, gestures for me to move over and stretches on the table, next to me.

"Do you think dad is up there?" he asks, resting his head on my shoulder.

"I don't know." I'm suddenly struggling for breath.

"I mean do you think he's in heaven?"

"I'd like to think he's some place nice, buddy."

"Do you think he can see us?"

He jerks himself up, lifts his hand and waves frantically.

"Hey, Dad! Hope you are having a good time up there!"

"I'm sure he -," It's all I can manage.

He settles back in and wraps his hands around me. The clouds gather. Misshaped blobs cover the stars.

"Look," he points up. "That cloud looks like a tiger. The head. Four paws and the tail.

"Yeah," I hug him back tight. "And that one, like a big fat whale!"

Image by Unknown Artist
Public domain

REBELS

Don't move?
Don't go?
Stay in line?
Wait on the line?
Follow the path?

Not us! Never us!
We pave the new roads
where no one walked before.
We sow our gardens
in rough and fruitless soil.

Nurturing our ideas
we follow them through
and colour your black-and-white existence
in bold colours.
Red on the green, yellow on blue,

we re-draw the blueprints of your measured life.
We push the boundaries
And map-out our lives far and wide.
Rebels! Libertines! You scream at us today.
In years to come, what will your children call us?

Image by Dee Mulrooney*

13.1 – ONLY HALF CRAZY

Foamy mountains grow around the waterfall cascading from the tap.

My sweat soaked clothes are piled up in the corner. With a smile of a happy idiot, I sit on the side of the bath. Naked. "13.1 – I'm Only Half crazy" says the slogan of my wet top. I would argue with that. I think I'm a total nut case.

I measure a generous portion of Epson salts into a bath and stir with my hand.

The water is steaming, in contrast, to the side of the bathtub that I'm sitting on. It's cold. Refreshing. Despite the freezing temperatures outside, I'm face and body flushed. Too hot. Too tired. Can barely move.

When the water reaches the level and the bathroom mirror disappears in the hot mist, I step in. My knees are locked, every move is a torture.

I suspend myself above the bath on my hands and ease my exhausted body in. A sigh of relief mixed with pain runs through the foamy mountains, as water stings every chafed part, every blister and each of my lovely toes that has just sustained a continuous hammering against the pavement for the period of 2 hours, 42 minutes, and 15 seconds.

As I soak in the heat penetrating deep into my muscles, my phone buzzes on the side. It's my running buddy. Today was her first Half too. We ran, socially distanced, of course, 50 miles apart, but together in spirit.

"How are you?" flashes on the screen.

I reply with a picture of my pedicured toes peeking from under the abundance of the bath bubbles.

"You?"

She sends me a smiley face and a photo. A view of a pointy knees sticking out from the bubble-bath and a foam-covered hand holding a peanut butter and banana sandwich.

"Yum!" I reply, glancing at the bathroom stand which hosts my cup of coffee and half eaten sandwich.

"How are you feeling?"

"Dead! In Pain! Excited!" I shoot one message after another. "But honestly, so chuffed! Can't believe we've actually done it!"

"Me too! So proud of us!"

"Never again though!"

"Never!"

I sit in a bath until the water grows cold and my children start banging on the door telling me they want lunch.

Wincing in pain, I heave myself out of the bath, pull on a bath robe and stagger into the hall on the straight legs. I stand for some time by the staircase, thinking I should probably camp downstairs, on the couch, until my legs recover.

Phone buzzes in my pocket.

"Farnborough half in 3 months?"

"Are you crazy? We just done one!"

"Only Half crazy, remember?"

"Half crazy it is!"

* **Dee Mulrooney** *is an emerging Irish artist, living and working in Berlin.*
Raised working-class in a small nation dominated by Catholicism and men, she now lives as a teacher, a mother, and an artist discovering the joy of playing with taboos and visions of female identity that would until all to recently have seen her locked away.
Her projects span visual art, film, storytelling, and theatre.
deemulrooney@gmail.com; IG: @deemulrooney

SWEET BACON (OR TRY NOT TO SING)

Image by Tom or Judy Moore*

Where do I start?
I can't believe it's been so long.
Nearly a year has gone,
and our feelings are growing strong.

I struggled in lockdown
then it became a norm.
Who would have thought
you'd come along!

Snouts
Touchin' screens
Oinkin' out
Texting me
Texting youuuuu

O my sweet pig! (ta-da-da)
Loving you never felt so gooooood
Your sweet bacon
Is putting me in a playful mood.

Now I look at my life
and it no longer feels so lonely.

Despite restrictions and lockdown
our love still grows on so lovely

And when I'm alone
feeling the weight of the world on my shoulders
I reach out to you
and there's no more pain!

Hooves
Touchin' screens
Reachin' out
Texting me
Texting youuuuu

O my sweet pig! (ta-da-da)
Loving you never felt so gooooood
Your sweet bacon
Is putting me in a playful mood.

*__Judy Moore__ is a multifunctional artist and busy little bee. She has exhibited widely including at the National Portrait Gallery, the ICA, The Freud Museum, Whose Museum and the Museum of Communication Berlin. Her trans memoir comic Everything is Somewhat Repaired won the Berlin Senate Comics Stipend in 2023.
IG: @ignatzhoch

VROOM-VROOM-BANG-BANG!

Image by Marie-Michèle Bouchard
Public domain

"Vroom! Vroom!" Rocking in his wheelchair, Jake makes a grabbing motion with his hands.

I smile and pass him two little diecast models.

"Bang! Bang!" he shouts, crushing them heads on.

The motion is on repeat, over and over again, until both vehicles are just a mash of metal and paint. He then drops them onto the floor, into a slowly growing pile of scrap metal cars and looks up at me.

"Vroom? Vroom?"

On autopilot, I unbox a new pair and hand it over to him. His high-pitch scream pierces my ears, as I note that one of the cars is an ambulance.

"I'm sorry buddy! I am so sorry." I reach for a new box.

"Autistic. Non-verbal," said the doctors.
"It will be alright," you assured me. "After all, we're a team."

And for some time, we were just that – a team. Until one day you've decided you've had enough, and started taking longer hours at work, just to be out of the house for as long as you could.

"Vroom. Vroom," Jake would repeat, sitting up late by the bay window, waiting for your car's headlights to flood the driveway.

"Vroom! Vroom!" he'd scream if I tried to put him to bed before you were back home.

Long hours at work progressed into weekends away, social things, networking or hanging out with your mates, until one day you've just packed your things, shoved the suitcase in the boot of your car and slammed the door.

"Vroom! Vroom!" Jake ran after you into the dark street, as you revved the engine and reversed to come out of the driveway.

You didn't see him. You were too angry to see anything. But that's not what you said to the police; you blamed the council and the broken streetlights. You didn't blame me, which was new.

Ambulance arrived within ten minutes and took Jake away. Total strangers showed your son more love and compassion than you ever did.

What followed after, were the long hours of surgery and recovery, witness statements and court hearings and you making empty promises and begging me to lie for you. After all, we were a team.

I scoop Jake up from his wheelchair. His hands lock strong around my neck, but his legs hang limp as if he's a rag doll. We go through the evening routine and settle for the night. I crawl into his small bed, cradling him in my arms.

"Vroom. Vroom," he mumbles, slowly drifting off to sleep, a small ambulance pressed tight against his chest.

"Yes, my darling," I whisper into his hair. "Vroom, vroom."

Image by Maria Victoria Rodriguez*

RUSSIAN SOUL

Misunderstood
unmeasured
vast as the fields of precious rye,
deep as the wilderness of taiga forests
that run from Europe to the Chinese borders,
that's borderless like the cloudless sky.

Serene
yet fierce
it's kind, blue-eyed and blond-haired.
It's raised on fairy-tales of Pushkin's learned cat,
that walks upon the chain around the mighty oak,
on songs and balalaika tunes that played by village folk.

Forced out
to a foreign country
it yearns for a piece of home. It searches
but cannot settle and weeps by the tallest birch
for a life that once there was,
dreaming of banya, vodka, garmon' i losos'.

***Maria Victoria Rodriguez García** – Argentina born, Germany based multitalented artist. Maria Victoria creates amazing bright and colourful posters.
IG: @mvictoria.rodriguez

IT'S NEVER TOO LATE TO PACK UP AND GO TO MEET YOUR TRUEST SELF

Image by Jim Pickerell/Documerica
Public domain

You stand in the middle of the road, rain washing over you, your hands are too loaded with heavy baggage to reach for an umbrella. Your life is steady. Comfortable. Carefully planned according to the standards pre-approved by the society. First – a career and jumping onto the property ladder, working yourself to the bone and partying with friends like there's no tomorrow. Then – a family and losing yourself to motherhood. Perhaps a divorce and a depression, a new hobby, a fling with a yoga teacher or a horse-riding instructor, a retirement at sixty-five, a cruise around the world and death. And somewhere along the pre-programmed "to do" that's expected of you, you've lost that precious connection with yourself. Lying in bed at night, you can't help but wonder "what if". "What if I could?" "What if I would?" Hesitating to take the step into the unknown. Convinced it's already too late. And then one morning you wake up. Wake up to the sound of the same rain still raging outside feeling somewhat different. New. Refreshed. But most importantly free. A new you jumps out of bed; she puts on a blue dress with a yellow belt, grabs a rainbow-striped bag and a pink coat and heads into the rain armed with a coral red umbrella. It shoots up, spreading its wings above your head. Your kaleidoscope of colours brightens up a grey day. People stare. Some smile. Some shake their heads, but you don't care. No longer hesitant, you raise your hand and pull in a taxi.

"Where to?" asks the driver. Your symphony of colours makes him squint.

"To the new me, please."

He nods and starts the engine.

You climb into the car and sink into the back seat.

Bob Marley's life-reassuring hymn pours from the radio.

SWEET DREAMS
(TO MY SONS)

I closed my eyes and walked into a dream
that's full of giants and the magic creatures.

I rode a dragon-shaped white, bearded snake
and danced along the length of rainbow bridges.

I strolled the sponge-soft banks of milk and kissel rivers
then built a raft of candy-canes and travelled up the stream.

I sailed the seven seas to find the pirates' treasures
then flew up to the moon and touched the silver beam.

I slayed three-headed beast and saved a princess charming.

She softly kissed my head and whispered to my ear
with the voice so soft, it sounded like mummy's:

"Good night, sleep tight, my darling,
and have the sweetest dreams."

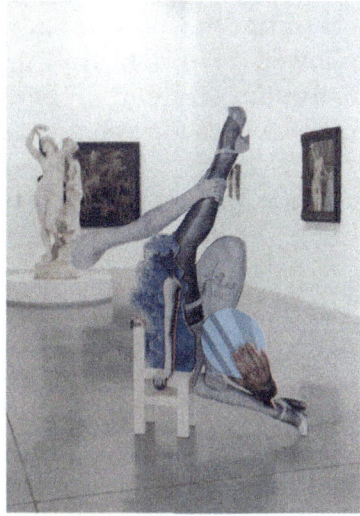

FEEDING HUNGRY MINDS

Image by Valérie Mannaerts/M Museum Leuven/Alexandra Colmenares. Public domain

The coach pulls in, and eighty-seven eager nine-year-olds pour into the street.

Head-counted, divided into the groups and assigned a responsible adult to keep a track of their whereabouts during the trip, they're navigated through the busy Exhibition Road, around the corner, and into the group entrance of the most exciting places in London.

Once all the questions about an earlier lunch or a pre-lunch snack have been addressed, we begin our ascent to the sanctuary of knowledge. Plunged into the white noise of the children's lively conversations, occasionally reaching the painful level of 150 decibels, we, unknowingly, become the subjects of the first experiment of the day.

At the top floor, we're greeted by a theatrically enthusiastic girl with the signs of late-night partying on her face, eyes and in her hoarse voice, which she strains trying to bring the storm of overexcited children to order.

"And so, unlike in other museums," she finishes, energetically clasping her hands in front of her chest, "where you're not allowed to touch anything, or to step over the red line, in our Superlab you can do all these things! Touch, feel, experiment. In other words – have fun! Any questions?"

"When are we going to have lunch?" asks a shy voice from the back.

The girl smiles and steps away, letting the children into the lab. Knowledge-hungry, each group explodes in through the narrow entrance and, like particles suspended in gas, moves around the perimeter in a Brownian-like motion.

Some forty-five minutes later, having satisfied their first craving for learning, kids are sitting on the floor in a circle, tiredly looking at a young man dressed in a museum shirt, who, acting out the meaning of the word "explainer" printed on his back, is shouting into his headset, explaining the principles of electricity.

"Why is electricity important and what do we use it for? Apart from playing Fortnite and Minecraft, of course. Yes, young man."

"To play Roblox!" comes the confident answer.

The logic is hard to argue and, by-and-by, the Explainer agrees that electricity is, indeed, essential for playing PS4 and charging iPhone and a tablet, and proceeds with a demonstration of a giant Tesla coil.

"Amazing, isn't it? 1 million volts! Any questions?"

"Is it lunch time yet?" flies in from the different sides.

Leaving the Superlab, armed with question-sheet and pencils, grumpy and moaning hungry children scout the space section of the museum, until, finally, happy and content, for the first time since the beginning of the trip, they are seated at the terrace, munching their sandwiches, crisps and fruits, sharing jokes and memories of chemistry bar, a colour room and friction slides.

At 3:20pm, tired but happy, we return to school. I peel off the "helper" sticker from my shirt, sign my child off and together we walk home.

"Did you have fun today?"

"Yes!" he declares, happily hopping next to me.

"What was your favourite part?"

"Lunch!"

DIVING FOR GOLD

Image by Olga Naida
Public domain

These waters are treacherous,
but there's gold, deep down at
the very bottom, lying in wait,
wanting to be rediscovered.

I gear up – mask, weights, flippers – and dive.

These waters are treacherous
swarming with predators –
Lies, Gossip, Hurt, Abuse, Judgment.
They bind my legs, restrain my hands,

hold me suspended, floundering in these mucky waters.

But there're treasures, the most
precious of them all, buried deep,
lying in wait, longing to be rediscovered –
Love, Faith, Kindness, Compassion, Hope.

I hold my breath and dive deeper searching for gold.

REAL KNIGHTS DON'T WEAR SHINING ARMOUR

Image by Unknown Artist (circa 1560) / Getty Open Content Program
Public domain

Sweating heavily under the summer hat, I push the buggy with my sleeping two-year-old down the garden pathway, while Max, my four-year-old, is galloping around us on his hobby horse wielding his wooden sword.

Despite the scorching heat, Hampton Court is swarming with visitors. They are streaming through the garden paths from all the different directions towards the farthest side of the grounds fenced off for jousting tournament.

Through the mighty trees, Max can already see the tents and horses and mimics their loud neighing, and I pray that the smell of manure wafting around doesn't give him any ideas.

We make our way through the crowd and make a picnic under one of the mighty trees next to a German couple in their seventies, who seem as excited as Max. He bubbles to them about his horse and offers them a ride. The old gentleman mounts a stick and pretends to gallop. His wife giggles. Max booms with laughter. I smile and nod, gratefully.

The trumpets blow and the noise dies down. The Royal Jester delivers a greeting, and everyone cheers for King Henry the VIII and his wife as they make their way to the throne placed inside the medieval pavilion tent. I can't hear the King's address as my two-year-old is now fully awake and fussing and Max is having a tantrum over the bowl of grapes his hobby horse just knocked over. The German couple distracts him, pointing at the real horses dressed in a full-on gear in the colours of the jousting knights. The latter are clad in metal, and I wonder if they ain't gonna drown there in their own sweat, as I am clearly struggling even in my light summer dress.

The trumpets go on again and the horses move to the opposite sides of the court. Knights position their lances. Horses rear and break into a gallop. Crowd sighs in disappointment as there was no contact. Second time is the miss again, but on the third attempt the lances crash, wood exploding into tiny splinters. One of the knights flies off the back of his horse. The crowd cheers.

Fanfares played and the winner is presented to the King. The knight takes off his helmet and flashes a smile. His long locks cascade onto his shoulders and I begin to fan myself with a hem of my skirt.

Someone taps my shoulder. It's my husband. He's a train driver and runs Waterloo to Hampton Court train thirty-five hours a week. He's not a prince charming – not shaven, slightly overweight, in a wrinkled shirt. He kisses our youngest, scoops the older one into his arms and tosses him into the air. Max squeals with delight. He sets him down, puts his arm around me and brushes his lips against mine. I nest my head on his chest. He's in desperate need of a haircut but I can't help but wonder how he will look with a longer hair.

UNTIL WE MEET AGAIN

Image by Unknown Artist / Getty
Open Content Program
Public domain

As days went by, I watched you slip away.
The golden fire in your eyes grew cold and turned ashen-grey.

The silken smoothness of your skin and softness of your voice
was snatched away from me too soon. I wish we had a choice.

The days flew by, the years have gone, the centuries have
passed. Yet still I grieved my timeless loss, your love still held
me fast.

Forever cursed to walk alone I travelled far and wide. Yet still, I
craved your gentle touch, and all we've left behind.

Millennia have come and gone, I fed my urge and lust, and then
one day, when I despaired, we met again. At last!

A simple square of wood and paint preserved your sacred light.
Your soft brown eyes, shy curve of lips still smiled to my delight.

And so I come to this museum to sit by your portrait
To live and hope, to hope and wait, until we meet again.

MINUTES OF THE EXTRAORDINARY MEETING OF THE "CLAWS AND WHISKERS SOCIETY"

Image by Erica Marsland Huynh
Public domain

Minutes of the Extraordinary Meeting of the "Claws and Whiskers Society" held on the 01.06.2023 at 1am.

Present:

Luna and Jarvis, Tobias, Jamuna, Oscar, Branston, Hermes, Ozzy, Valentino and Beatrice, Belle and Bailey, Willow, Floki, Felix, and Vinny.

* it was noted that due to the emergency of the matter, a notice of a meeting wasn't served through the usual channels, but circulated at a short notice through a word of mouth and some of the members of the Society weren't able to attend.

Luna and Jarvis, a sweet old couple that they are, have offered to host the meeting at their garden, which was a great change from a usual hang out at the construction site. They have also promised light snacks and offered to make use of their heated garden jacuzzi.

The purpose of the meeting was to discuss the arrival to the Estate of a new Egyptian couple (with so very un-Egyptian names) – CoCo and Cosmo, who probably think themselves to be some sort of royalty but are feral beasts if I can say so myself! Anyway, to the task at hand.

Jamuna noted that the newcomers have moved in less than four days ago and have already managed to cause havoc among the local residents.

Branston agreed that they have shown absolutely no respect to boundaries of private property.

Willow whispered that last night she'd caught them snooping in her garden.

Oscar said that he had to chase them away as they tried to raid his bird house, probably scaring the little hatchlings to death.

It was eventually agreed by the attendees that something had to be done, the sooner the better.

Hermes offered to speak with Cosmo man-to-man.

Vinny, the oldest on the Estate, said she didn't understand what all the fuss was about and reminded everybody of their own behaviour when they only moved in. She also added that she finds CoCo very stylish.

Valentino and Beatrice had spent most of the time cuddling, rubbing their noses, and doing all sorts of inappropriate things on the bench. I understand she's pregnant, but why on earth had they bothered to come in the first place!

At about 4am, they have made their way home, taking with them their offspring's Belle and Bailey - who also haven't had any input in a meeting.

With them gone, everyone cozied up on a warm cover of jacuzzi. Youngsters Floki and Felix sneaked into the house through the purposefully ajarred window and dragged out a few slices of pizza and chicken wings.

When the party started to get out of hand, Luna and Jarvis's owner shouted at us from the window things that are too dramatic to be put in the minutes and threw a pair of crocs at our company.

The participants have scattered, and the meeting was adjourned.

Signed and logged into the minute book of the Society, by the Chairman and a Secretary:

/Tobias Crawford/
aka His Furriness, Toby the Stripy Pants.

STALKER

I stalk you.
Following your every step,
I watch your life evolve
before my very eyes.

I hide behind
the corner of each page and drink
your full existence, savouring your
world like it's the rarest wine.

I watch you
run your fingers through her silky hair,
caress her face, and seal your lips
with hers.

Like a criminal,
I'm lurking in the shadows
of the room, as you make love,
and wish that I was her.

Pierced by the rival's sword,
I see you fall and bleed.
I hold my breath and pray,

afraid to turn the page to find that you are dead.

I close the book,
my fingers linger over the cover of the treasured leather bind.
You do not even know that I exist, yet our lives
entwined.

THE WEEPING OF A BRIDE*

Image by John Everett Millais/Birmingham Museums Trust. Public domain

"Oh, but forests above the Volga River are as green as emeralds,
Oh, but the warm spring winds are blowing above the arable
lands..."

And she stares at the clouds gathered up far away,
knowing now that her life never will be the same,

for the boy that she loves is out of grasp, out of reach,
and the man she's to wed – well, he is old and he's rich.

Just the trees in the woods and the birds in the field
know how broken her heart that will never be healed.

And the willow that weeps and the river that flows
hear the toll of church's bells and the call of the crows.

As thunder breaks out, splitting the sky overhead,
the bright rainbow comes out – promise of good times ahead.

And she lifts up her face, letting tears to roll free,
rain clears off her pain, set her soul to be free.

"Oh, but forests above the Volga River are as green as emeralds, Oh but the warm spring winds are blowing above the arable lands..."

* Inspiration for this piece came from an old Russian folklore tradition. In the old times, when the village girls would be married off, as a part of the wedding tradition, they would sing a sad song (pretty much crying and complaining about being married off to the man they don't love) as they are being dressed and prepared for the ceremony. The official name of the song/process in traditional folklore is "the weeping of a bride". I had a chance to see a re-creation of the tradition and thought it was very beautiful and moving.

ONCE IN A BLOOD MOON

Image by Kitty Harrison x Dylan Sauerwein
Public domain

Rays of the setting sun prismed through Karen's half-empty whiskey glass. She glanced at her watch, then heaved a bag onto her shoulder, and hurried up the stairs.

In the little attic room with a small roof window facing the east, two floor mirrors were already placed a few metres apart, one opposite the other.

She hesitated for a second; a panic from realisation of what she was about to do ran a cold shiver down her spine, but there was no turning back now. The room was slowly plunging into the dark.

Karen tipped the contents of the bag onto the table. Five big black candles, two tall white candles, two smudge bowls, two bunches of wormwood, one bunch of sage. There was also a moonstone ring that she inherited from her grandmother. She's been wearing it all week. That's what the Medium, Madam Rosalinda, said she must do to charge the stone with the energy.

Karen dragged the chair into the middle of the room, right

between the mirrors. She placed the black candles on the floor, in the high corners of the imaginary pentagram, and the white candles by the front mirror, the smudge bowls filled with wormwood on the sides of the chair. Madam Rosalinda was very specific in her instructions.

Once the moon began to peek through the roof window, Karen lit the candles and the wormwood, and sat on the chair, a bunch of sage and a lighter clutched tightly in her hands, her gaze fixed on her own endless reflections.

Slowly, the red moon filled the window. Its shimmering light poured into the room, bouncing off the moonstone on her finger, mixing with the flickering light of the candles, filling the dark abyss of the mirrors with a gentle glow.

It might be that her eyes were beginning to tire, but the shadows in the depth of the mirror began to move. Then, she heard light footsteps. Then, a soft giggle. And then a little boy walked towards her from the darkness.

Karen froze, her heart thumping in her ears. He looked different to what she last remembered him. Not in a hospital gown, not bald with sunken cheeks and dark circles under his eyes. Bright-eyed, with rosy cheeks, he wore a red coat, the one she bought him when he was five.

The boy played hopscotch within the boundaries of the mirrors, then sat on the floor as if playing with the toys only he could see.

He was so close. She could feel him. She could probably touch him, if she reached out, but Madam Rosalinda was very strict. Karen didn't move and kept her gaze forward, eyes stinging with tears.

As the moon left the window, the light of the moonstone faded away and so did the image of the boy. Karen lit up the bunch of sage and sat in the dark until the early hours of the morning.

Image by Vony Razom
Public domain

WALPURGIS NIGHT

When the Queen, blood moon, rises
and her court of diamond stars shine
brightly from their black velvety palace,

they leave their boyfriends, husbands
and their children, sneak out from the
open windows and fly to the top of

the Lysaya Gora - the Bald Mountain.

Under-loved, underappreciated, they
gather in their thousands. Lighting
the fires of their dreams, they burn

herbs. They sing songs and dance in circles.
Naked. With hula-hoops and tambourines.
Channelling their inner goddesses.

Somewhat lost. Somewhat forgotten.

In the dark waters of the blood river,

they re-capture the true reflection of their beings.
Goddesses. Powerful. Fearless.

of all the ages, colours, shapes, and sizes.
Rejuvenated, they return at dawn,
to be once again

girlfriends, wives, and mothers.

Image by Marc Schlossman
Public domain

WEIGHING OUT THE OPTIONS

It's a lazy Sunday afternoon. I'm chilling in a hammock, enjoying the gentle warmth of an early October sun as it leisurely rolls over yet still lush green lawn.

My first born, now a teenager, is sprawled on the inflatable mattress in a shady part of the garden, armed with a notepad, pen and his phone. Long blond curls frame his too serious face, and I can't help but wonder when did I blink, and my baby turned into this handsome young man. He's still the goofiest of the goofs, still writes letters to Santa and still allows me to hug him in public, but there's a new sense of manhood about him. He scrolls through his phone, makes notes, then crosses out what he's just written, blows out the air through his mouth and scratches his head.

It's love, you see. The kind that sweeps you off your feet and possesses you body and soul.

It took time but he traced her to a small music shop 45-min-train-journey-away. It was the closest he could find to the one that Metallica's frontman has. Hanging on the back wall of the shop, apple red with golden shimmer, it came with a heavy price tag, but it was love at first sight, sealed forever with first riff.

"How's it going?" I ask.

He gives me the look.

"Even if I save ALL my pocket money, cut the grass every 4 weeks, do the bins, do all my chores, be exceptionally good at school and get tons of house points, I'll still only be able to afford it in about two and a half years." He frowns. "Are you sure you can't help me with that?"

"No, buddy. It's all on you."

"Right. Right." He scratches his head again and disappears into the house.

He reappears a few minutes later with brain food – a bag of Haribos, two packs of crisps and a can of coke – and continues to scroll through his phone making notes and adding numbers, crossing them out and then starting again.

"What if you buy it for me and I'll pay you back?" he asks cautiously.

"Within two and a half years?"

"No way, right?" He cackles. "Worth an ask, eh?"

He gets serious again then lift his eye up to me.

"I can sell my Pokémon card or NERF guns collection!"

"Will you really?"

He shakes his head, energetically.

"Well, there's always a backup option," he says as a matter of fact.

"Which is?"

"I'll ask Santa!" he grins. "I'm really, REALLY good at school, I tolerate my brother, and help with the cat and stuff. The old man loves me. He always gets me what I ask for!" he adds with a devilish curve of a brow.

"Yeah." I gulp, slowly. "About that."

About Ekaterina

Ekaterina is a poet and a writer.

She was born and grew up in Russia but relocated to the UK with her husband in 2006.

She always loved writing but it's only in the past few years that she's really pursued her passion.

Over the years, many of her creative pieces were published by the Visual Verse Online Anthology. She won Poetry (2021) and Short Story (2022) Competitions in Writers' Forum Magazine and was placed first in a Romance Category in Farnham Literary Festival Short Story Competition in 2022.

She had a poem shortlisted and two other works published by the Bournemouth Writing Prize Anthologies 2022.

In 2022, her war poem "Bucha" reached the top 12% (the long list) of Bridport Poetry Prize entries.

She has published time travel romantic adventure "Sherwood Untold: The Journey" (Book 1 of a Trilogy) and "800 Years Apart" a short spin-off story from the Sherwood Untold series, both inspired by the BBC's Robin Hood TV show.

Ekaterina is currently working on many short stories and book two of the Sherwood Untold series.

She lives in Hampshire with her family.

Other books by Ekaterina Crawford

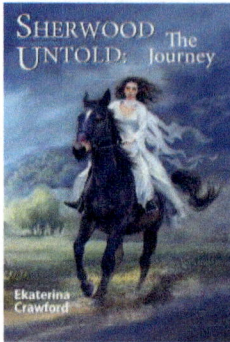

She is a successful barrister who revolves in high society and leads a comfortable, happy life in London. He is a ruthless murderer, the right-hand man and Commander-in-Chief to the callous Sheriff of Nottingham. However, looks are often deceptive and behind the strong façade, there hides a broken and lonely soul, longing for compassion, happiness and love.

The old Robin Hood story with an original twist, Sherwood Untold: The Journey is a time-travelling, romantic adventure that takes you from modern London back to medieval England, to the times of King Richard the First, Robin Hood and the Sheriff of Nottingham.

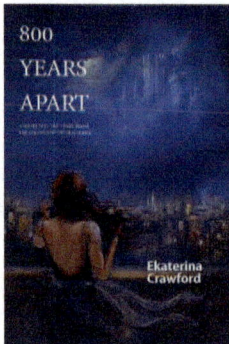

800 Years Apart, is a short spin-off story from the Sherwood Untold series that gives a glimpse into the life of Christine Hawk, the series main character, after she had to leave an injured Guy of Gisborne behind, in Medieval England, and return home, back to her own time.

The Ninth Gate Publishing

Books That Take You Places

Printed in Great Britain
by Amazon